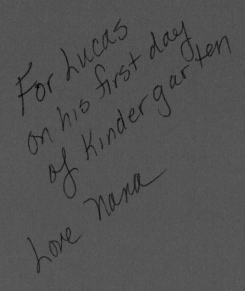

For Lucas
on his first day
of Kindergarten

Love Nana

On the First Day

of Kindergarten

To my grandsons, Cole and Chase, with love — T.R.

For Little Eddie — L.H.

On the First Day

# of Kindergarten

by Tish Rabe pictures by Laura Hughes

HARPER
An Imprint of HarperCollinsPublishers

On the first day of kindergarten

I thought it was so cool

riding the bus to my school!

On the second day of kindergarten

I thought it was so cool

making lots of friends

and riding the bus to my school!

On the third day of kindergarten

I thought it was so cool

counting up to ten,

making lots of friends,

and riding the bus to my school!

On the fourth day of kindergarten
I thought it was so cool

running in a race,

counting up to ten,

making lots of friends,

and riding the bus to my school!

On the fifth day of kindergarten
I thought it was so cool

SINGING A SONG!

running in a race,

counting up to ten,

making lots of friends,

and riding the bus to my school!

On the sixth day of kindergarten
I thought it was so cool

sliding down the slide,

SINGING A SONG!
running in a race,
counting up to ten,
making lots of friends,
and riding the bus to my school!

On the seventh day of kindergarten

I thought it was so cool

sorting by shapes,

sliding down the slide,

SINGING A SONG!

running in a race,

counting up to ten,

making lots of friends,

and riding the bus to my school!

On the eighth day of kindergarten
I thought it was so cool
sharing a story,

sorting by shapes,
sliding down the slide,
SINGING A SONG!
running in a race,
counting up to ten,
making lots of friends,
and riding the bus to my school!

On the ninth day of kindergarten
I thought it was so cool
painting a picture,

sharing a story,
sorting by shapes,
sliding down the slide,
SINGING A SONG!
running in a race,
counting up to ten,
making lots of friends,
and riding the bus to my school!

On the tenth day of kindergarten
I thought it was so cool
laughing at lunch,

painting a picture,
sharing a story,
sorting by shapes,
sliding down the slide,
SINGING A SONG!
running in a race,
counting up to ten,
making lots of friends,
and riding the bus to my school!

On the eleventh day of kindergarten

I thought it was so cool

jumping rope in gym,

laughing at lunch,

painting a picture,

sharing a story,

sorting by shapes,

sliding down the slide,

SINGING A SONG!

running in a race,

counting up to ten,

making lots of friends,

and riding the bus to my school!

On the twelfth day of kindergarten

I thought it was so cool

going on a field trip,

jumping rope in gym,

laughing at lunch,

painting a picture,

sharing a story,

sorting by shapes,

sliding down the slide,

SINGING A SONG!

running in a race,
counting up to ten,
making lots of friends,

AND RIDING THE BUS TO MY SCHOOL!